The Two Sisters

by
Terri Dawn Arnold

TDA
Entertainment
Inc.

The Two Sisters
crime / drama / mystery

Chapter 1

Susan

Susan stands at the kitchen sink washing dishes before cooking dinner. She can hear Lannie and Kellie in their room. They should be doing their homework, but Susan is too tired after working a double shift to check.

Thirty-two-year-old Susan looks older than her age. Her life has continuous hardships. Since giving birth to her oldest daughter Lannie 14 years ago, she has been forced to do the best she can to make it on her own. Her dream of becoming a professional dancer is a fantasy from her childhood that was so long ago. Her youngest daughter Kellie is 13 years old, coming along just one year after

Lannie, and causing her father to leave Susan just as Lannie's father did.

As Susan places a pot on the stove and turns on the heat, Paul walks into the apartment. She has been dating Paul for five months. She vividly remembers how she met him one morning on her way to work. After dropping the girls at school, she recalls making an unusual stop for coffee on a day when her energy was depleted.

"I'm in here," said Susan.

Paul walks into the kitchen carrying a bag.

"Where have you been?"

"I went to the store. You said you wanted sodas," said Paul.

"Why are you always leaving?"

Paul becomes annoyed and puts the bag on the table.

"What's wrong with you?"

"There's nothing wrong with me. You're the problem!"

"You know, Susan, I've had it. I'm not takin' this abuse from you anymore."

"Abuse! What abuse?"

"Once again, you're in denial. I'm tired of this! One minute you're depressed and the next you're hostile."

Paul turns and walks towards the door. Susan follows him.

"Where are you going?"

Because of the yelling, Susan's daughters walk down the hall. They stare into the living room, listening and watching Susan and Paul without being seen or heard.

Paul turns towards Susan.

"I'm leaving," said Paul.

"You can't leave!"

"Watch me."

Paul turns around once again, walking through the living room and towards the front door. Susan runs up behind Paul, jumping on his back and tightly wrapping her arms around him.

"What are you doing?"

Paul pushes Susan off his body and she falls. Her head hits the coffee table. Paul walks out of the apartment and Lannie and Kellie run into the living room screaming, crying, and shaking their

mother but receiving no response from her.

Chapter 2

Uncle Nathan

Lannie and Kellie are crying and standing by their Uncle Nathan's side at their mother's grave. Nathan looks at the girls.

"You're going to live with your Aunt Joanie, Little Nathan, and me now. You should not be afraid. Paul will be in jail for a long time."

Lannie and Kellie each take their uncle's hand and walk away from their mother's grave.

One summer afternoon Lannie sits on the living room couch of Nathan's house reading a magazine while Kellie and Little Nathan play a video game.

"Stop cheating Nathan," said Kellie.

"I'm not cheating. You just don't know how to play," said Little Nathan.

"I *do* know how to play."

Little Nathan starts laughing at Kellie.

"No, you don't. You're stupid."

"What's funny? You little brat!"

"Would you both shut up," said Lannie.

"No! Make me," said Little Nathan.

Lannie jumps up and Little Nathan runs out of the room shouting.

"Mom! Lannie hit me!"

"I didn't hit him! I'm sick of that little…," said Lannie.

"I know, me too," said Kellie.

Aunt Joanie storms into the room.

"Lannie! Did you hit Little Nathan?"

"What do you think?"

"I'm going to ask you one more time. Did you hit Little Nathan?"

"What does it matter? You're not going to believe me anyway."

"That's it! I'm calling your uncle."

Aunt Joanie walks out of the room. Little Nathan smiles and sticks his tongue out at Lannie while following his mother. Lannie and Kellie follow Aunt Joanie into the kitchen where she picks up the telephone. Lannie grabs Aunt Joanie around the neck and starts choking her until she stops breathing. Kellie watches. Uncle Nathan walks into the house and picks up the mail sitting on the table in the foyer.

"Hi, I'm home. Where is everybody?"

Uncle Nathan walks into the kitchen where he sees Lannie and Kellie standing over Aunt Joanie.

"Oh my God, what happened?"

Little Nathan is crying, yelling, and pointing at Lannie and Kellie.

"They did it!"

Nathan commits Lannie and Kellie to Standard Sanitarium. This is what he tried to avoid. He impatiently waits for Doctor Henderson while completing enrollment forms with Nurse Louise. He is physically in the room, but his mind wanders, because he desperately misses his wife and is terrified for his son's safety. He convinces himself the decision to have his nieces placed in a psychiatric hospital is the right thing to do.

Doctor Henderson enters the room and shakes Nathan's hand before sitting down in a nearby chair.

"Mr. Ryan, I understand why you brought your nieces here, but are you sure this is what you want to do?"

"They killed . . . my wife. I have to protect my son."

"Of course . . . well, it appears that your nieces have a manic-depressive illness, also known as bipolar 1 disorder."

"My sister, their mother, was bipolar."

"It is genetic. Do you have any questions?"

"Not that I can think of right now."

"Okay, you have my card. You can contact me anytime."

Exiting the hospital, Nathan is apprehensive. An air of uncertainty flows through him. Normally, if someone's wife is killed, he seeks revenge, yet Joanie's killers are mentally unstable family members. Part of him hopes they receive the help they need. Another section of his brain tells him he should have done more to make sure they could never hurt anyone else.

Chapter 3

Standard Sanitarium

Five years later Lannie and Kellie are still living at Standard Sanitarium. Both girls have been taking lithium. They respond positively to the treatment they receive.

Lannie sits in her room staring at a picture of her mother. She expresses anger by tightening all muscles in her face. During her stay at Standard she spends many days in isolation. Discovering that she hates that, Lannie develops the body and facial contortions. This provides a liberating outlet for her and her anxiety is kept from others.

Kellie sleeps a lot, as she experiences sadness and confusion. She is depressed and often cries. Her focus is mourning her mother's death.

She believes the world is against her and responsible for taking her mother out of her life. But outside her room she is seen smiling.

In another area of the hospital, Dr. Henderson and Nurse Louise have a conversation about Lannie and Kellie. They disagree while walking down a hallway. Other hospital personnel can sense the tension in their discussion and pass by quickly.

"I cannot believe Lannie and Kellie Ryan are being released today," said Louise.

"Why should they stay here," asked Dr. Henderson.

"They appear to be better, and Kellie has made much more progress than Lannie. But I still do not think they should be released. They're not ready."

"Well, I think they are. And as long as they continue taking the prescribed medication, they should have no problems."

"That's just it, doctor. Will they continue taking the medication?"

Dr. Henderson becomes impatient with Nurse Louise.

"The responsibility is on them . . . and if you like your job Nurse Louise, I suggest you discontinue this conversation! Do I make myself clear?"

After saying this Dr. Henderson walks away and Nurse Louise is in disbelief.

Lannie and Kellie exit the building and step inside a taxi provided by Standard Sanitarium. Each has an expression of relief on her face, but a sense of confusion is also apparent. Lannie gives Uncle Nathan's address to the driver.

"We can't go back there," said Kellie.

"We're going," said Lannie.

"Why?"

"Just relax. You'll know what to do when we get there."

Kellie thinks Lannie's behavior is strange but does not question her again. Instead she stares out the window and views the world she had been detached from for five years.

The taxi driver stops in front of Uncle Nathan's house. Kellie notices a 'For Sale' sign.

She turns when she sees Lannie throwing her lithium prescription bottle out the window and it lands on Nathan's front lawn. Kellie smiles and then does the same. As their taxi drives away, Uncle Nathan walks outside the house carrying a box. He walks to the grass area close to the curb and picks up two full bottles of Lannie and Kellie's medications. He looks up, but the taxi has already turned the corner.

Chapter 4

California University

Today is 'move into the dorm day' at California University. Lannie and Kellie are the only students not being dropped off by parents or some other family members. Instead, the two sisters step out of a taxi and carry their belongings into the building they will now call home.

While at Standard, the girls remember the staff requiring them to attend classes and do homework. Life at a mental hospital does not mean children do not attend school. Both Lannie and Kellie are both good students and were encouraged by the Standard staff to apply to universities. The two sisters walk out of the elevator onto the third floor. They walk down the hall, searching for their room.

"I guess this is it. I can't wait to see inside our room," said Kellie.

"This *is* it," said Lannie.

People are walking down the hallway making noises. They all seem overjoyed about being away at college. As soon as their parents leave they yell, "Yeah!" A man, another freshman, walks by and smiles at Kellie.

"So far this seems like home," said Kellie."

Lannie raises her eyebrows at Kellie.

"Lannie, I want things to be different."

"What do you mean *different*?"

"This is our chance to make friends . . . and be normal."

Lannie ignores Kellie, the ladies enter the room, and Lannie starts unpacking.

Kellie nervously enters the lecture hall. She is excited about her first day of school at the university. She finds a seat in the middle of the room, which is a section no one else has filled in yet. But once she gets settled, more students begin sitting nearby. As soon as the professor walks into the lecture hall, everyone becomes silent. The instructor is a petite woman with long brown hair. She is not what Kellie imagined. Instead of an intimidating demeanor, she looks like a fashion model who may be easy to approach. Before addressing students, she writes on the board: 'Professor Davis. English 1.'

"In this course we will explore the various writing styles of several different authors."

Professor Renee' Davis pauses and gives the course syllabus to students.

"Please keep in mind, you are all full-time students. Your business is learning. I am handing out the syllabus for this semester and expect everyone to meet all requirements."

While Professor Davis talks to the class, Kellie sees the guy who smiled at her in the dorms. He is looking directly at her.

"Please turn to page two where you will find the reading list for the class. It is imperative that you obtain all texts and start reading immediately. Do not procrastinate. That is all for today."

Kellie walks out of the building and the very cute guy from the dorm approaches her.

"Hey! I'm Linc."

"Hi. I'm Kellie. What kind of name is Linc?"

Linc laughs and is unsurprised by Kellie's reaction to his name.

"It's short for Lincoln. My parents are very patriotic people."

"Oh, I get it."

"So, are you a freshman?"

"Yes. Are you?"

"Yeah."

"So, what do you think about this class?"

"She's tough. I've already been warned by some friends who took her class last year. Do you want to hang out sometime? We can study together."

"Sure. I live in Cadonian Dorms."

"I know! So do I. Later."

"Bye."

Kellie smiles as Linc walks away. She keeps looking at him until he is out of view.

Three women sit on a bench in the campus quad. Lannie sits nearby and observes.

"My birthday party is going to be the best," said Jessica.

"I can't wait," said Amy.

"Amy, I thought you had to work tonight," said Simone.

"You have a job," Jessica asked arrogantly.

Amy is humiliated. Simone turns to Amy.

"I'm sorry. I forgot I wasn't supposed to say anything," said Simone.

"So, where are you working," asked Jessica.

"At a salon," said Amy.

"Like, a day spa," asked Jessica.

"No, it's a hair salon," said Amy.

"They do manicures, too," said Simone.

"Oh, well I guess I'll have to stop by some time," said Jessica.

Jessica looks at her watch.

"Look what time it is. I've gotta go," said Jessica.

Jessica gets up and walks away.

"Bye Jessica," said Amy.

"I'm sorry. I didn't plan on saying anything. It just came out," said Simone.

"Well, now it's out. Jessica knows, and I'm sure she's going to tell Todd," said Amy.

"Why do you care if *he* knows?

"I don't know I just do. I'm really trying to fit in here. Jessica and most of the people at this school are rich and don't have to work."

Linc walks by Simone and Amy.

"Hello ladies," said Linc.

"Hi Linc," said Simone.

"Hi," Amy said demurely.

"That was your big chance. Why didn't you say more to him?

"I don't know," said Amy.

Amy places her head in her hands.

Lannie and Kellie sit beside each other at a table eating dinner in the dormitory dining commons. Lannie is dissatisfied, but Kellie is happy and in a good mood for the first time in a long time. Kellie realizes Lannie is not going to ask why she has chosen joy, so she enlightens her.

"I met a really nice guy today," said Kellie.

"You wanted to make friends. This food is terrible. I don't know how long I'm going to be able to stay in this place," said Lannie.

"Would you rather be back at Standard?"

"No. I'd actually like to be back at home."

"Standard was home. And the food was worse than this. Besides, Uncle Nathan sold the house."

"I don't care about him. I just want to live someplace else."

"Where?"

"I don't know yet. But as soon as I know I'll tell you. Do you want to go to a party?"

"Sure!"

Lannie and Kellie walk across campus to a sorority house. They hear the party before seeing the house. Every light inside is on and looking through the windows, the place is crowded.

As they enter the home, they realize even more that the house is extremely crowded, and music is playing loudly. A banner is hanging and states: "Happy Birthday Jessica." Kellie immediately sees Linc and Lannie sees her looking at him.

"Well, go over there," said Lannie.

"You don't mind," asked Kellie.

"No. Now go!"

"Okay."

Lannie, still standing near the door, stares at several people in the room. She wonders why she decided to crash Jessica's party. Suddenly, a tall, broad-shouldered man walks up to her.

"Hey. How's it goin'," asked Todd.

"I've been better," said Lannie.

"What's wrong? You're not having any fun?"

"I don't do small talk."

"Then what do you do?"

"Nothing with you."

Lannie walks away from Todd. She tries her best to ditch him. Todd is in shock. His friend, a fraternity brother named Jay, walks up to him.

"Who was that," asked Jay.

Todd is still looking in the direction that Lannie scurried.

"Someone who I'd love to get into," said Todd.

"What about Jessica?"

"What about her?"

"This is *her* party."

"So. I'm getting tired of her anyway. Everything is always about her."

As Todd walks away, Simone walks over to her boyfriend, Jay, and puts her arm around him. Todd manages to locate Lannie.

"Oh, you again," said Lannie.

"You can't get rid of me that easily," said Todd.

"You're persistent."

Jessica sees Todd talking to Lannie and walks over to them and pulls Todd's arm.

"Todd, come dance with me," said Jessica.

Todd pulls away from Jessica.

"Not now," said Todd.

Jessica touches Todd's arm again.

"I think *now* is a great time!"

Todd pulls away from Jessica again.

"Well, I don't!"

Lannie laughs. Jessica gives Lannie a mean look and furiously walks away. Lannie smiles. In another part of the room, Linc and Kellie talk.

"I'm glad you're here," said Linc.

"Me, too. My sister was invited to this party," said Kellie.

"I'll have to meet her."

Kellie points to the location where she last saw Lannie.

"She's over there."

"Talking to Todd?"

"Is that his name?"

"Yeah. We play football together."

"You play football?"

"Yeah."

"Do you have a scholarship?"

"Yes. How did you know?"

"Lucky guess. In high school I played softball. I could have gotten a scholarship."

"Why didn't you?"

"I haven't played in five years."

"What? You just said you played in high school."

Kellie really likes Linc but grows frustrated with his ongoing questions. She has lied about playing softball. Why couldn't he have just said, "Oh, really," and left it alone?

If he only knew the truth. Kellie did not attend regular high school. She took high school classes at Standard Sanitarium. There was no sports program. She was surrounded by crazy people and is mentally ill herself.

To avoid Linc discovering her lies, Kellie changes the subject.

"So, where are you from?"

Linc gets a weird look on his face and slightly laughs.

Amy sees Linc talking to Kellie. Simone notices Amy staring at Linc.

"Why don't you go talk to Linc," asked Simone.

"I just got here. And look, he's talking to someone," said Amy.

Amy is nervous and insecure. Jessica walks up to her and Simone.

"What are you guys talking about," asked Jessica.

"Amy was just about to go talk to Linc," said Simone.

"Yeah. I'm going to talk to Linc," said Amy.

Amy hesitates but walks away.

"Simone, do you see Todd," asked Jessica.

Simone looks around.

"No," said Simone.

Jessica points to where she left Todd.

"He's over there."

Simone looks around again.

"He must have left."

"No. He's talking to some girl."

Simone is in shock. Jessica and Todd are in their senior year and have been dating since they were freshmen. Jessica can be demanding, but Simone never expected Todd to cheat on her.

"Do you think he left with her?

Jessica starts crying.

"I don't know."

Lannie talks to Todd outside.

"You must be new here. I've never seen you before," said Todd.

"Do you have a problem with that," asked Lannie.

"Why are you so angry?"

"Do I seem angry to you?"

"Yeah, you sound pissed off."

Kellie walks outside with Linc. Amy stands back and watches.

"Lannie, this is Linc," said Kellie.

"Hi Lannie," said Linc.

"Hi," said Lannie.

"Hey Todd," said Linc.

"Hey," said Todd.

Todd introduces himself to Kellie.

"Linc is going to walk me back to the dorms," said Kellie.

"Okay," said Lannie.

Amy turns around and runs back into the house.

Lannie sees how happy Kellie is and shifts gears. She decides a little romance won't hurt her.

"You know Todd. . .I think you're right. I haven't been treating you very well," said Lannie.

Lannie moves closer to Todd.

"Do you want to go to my place? It's a frat house, but. . .," said Todd.

"Sure."

Kellie and Linc walk across campus. Before reaching the dorms, Linc gets serious.

"Kellie, I know we just met, but I really like you," said Linc.

Kellie smiles.

"I really like you, too," said Kellie.

"Cool."

"I thought you had a girlfriend."

"No way! What made you think that?"

"I saw the way those girls were looking at you at the party."

"Huh? I didn't notice. I don't even know any of them."

Kellie laughs. Linc is confused.

"I was just teasing you."

"Oh. Well, umm. . .can I kiss you?"

"Sure."

The two embrace and kiss.

In the morning the frat house is quiet. Todd is still asleep but wakes up when he hears movement. He sits up in bed and sees Lannie facing a mirror.

"It's morning. Do you still respect me," asked Todd.

"I was hoping to be gone before you woke up," said Lannie.

"I take that as a no."

"Bye Todd. It's been real."

Lannie walks out of the room. Todd is bewildered.

Kellie walks to class and sees Amy talking to Linc. It makes her angry, so she charges toward them.

"Do you think the class is hard," asked Amy.

"No, not at all. There's just a lot of work," said Linc.

"I noticed that, too. Maybe. . ."

"Hi Linc," said Kellie.

"Hi Kellie," said Linc.

"Who's this?"

Linc kisses Kellie on the cheek.

"This is Amy. Amy, this is Kellie."

Amy is frightened and barely speaks before walking away.

"I have to go. It was nice meeting you Kellie."

"You're leaving already," asked Kellie.

Kellie is envious of Amy. She feels an uncontrollable force inside of her but manages to hold herself back from acting on impulse.

"Do you like her?"

"She's okay," said Linc.

Kellie and Linc hold hands and walk to the lecture hall together.

After Professor Davis's lecture Kellie looks around the room and notices Amy is in the same class.

"Let's go for coffee," said Linc.

"No. I can't. I have to meet Lannie," said Kellie.

"Oh. Well, I'll call you later, okay?"

"Okay."

Kellie kisses Linc then walks up to the professor. Unsure of why she has told Linc she must meet Lannie, she nervously invents a concern she has about the course content.

"Professor Davis?"

"Yes," asked Professor Davis.

"I don't really understand what all the symbolism means in the short story we read."

"It's an allegory. Each character represents something. Do some critical thinking to discover what the writer is really trying to convey."

Kellie sees Amy and waits for her to walk by. This conversation buys her some time.

"Oh. Thank you."

Amy starts walking a little faster, but Kellie stops her.

"Amy!"

Amy turns around.

"Hi Kellie."

"Hi. Do you want to study together? This class is *very* tough."

"Wouldn't you prefer studying with Linc?"

"Don't get me wrong. Linc's a great guy, but I don't want to study with him *all* the time."

"Oh, I see."

"Do you have any time right now?"

Amy hesitates.

"I guess."

"Great! Let's go to the library."

"Okay."

Amy and Kellie start walking together. Amy is extremely uncomfortable. She stares at the ground a lot. Kellie scowls at Amy without her knowing it.

Inside the library Kellie interrogates Amy.

"Do you like Linc," asked Kellie.

"What do you mean," asked Amy.

Kellie grows impatient.

"Do you like him?"

"Do you mean as a person?"

"It is blatantly obvious that Linc is a nice person. I mean, do you want to do it with him?"

Amy is even more uncomfortable now than she was while walking to the library with Kellie.

"I thought he was going out with you."

"He is. Don't forget it!"

There is an awkward silence, then Kellie continues talking.

"You and I can still be friends."

Kellie smiles and Amy is shaken.

"Okay."

"What's wrong?"

"Nothing. This is just a weird conversation."

"You don't talk about guys?"

"I do. It's just. . ."

"Just what?"

"I don't know you very well."

"Do we have to know each other well to talk about guys?"

"I guess not."

"You never answered my question."

"What?"

"Do you want to do it with Linc?"

"No."

Kellie is unconvinced.

"But you do want to go out with him?"

"Not really."

"You're lying!"

Before Amy can respond, Kellie opens a book and continues speaking.

"Well, okay. Let's get started so we're not here all night."

Amy is perplexed. She does not understand the quick mood shift. Kellie's tone instantly changes.

Amy forces herself not to make eye contact with Kellie. She just stares at the book and listens to Kellie. When Kellie asks her a question, Amy holds back tears and indicates she is feeling sick, then gets up and leaves the library. As Amy walks away Kellie stares at her with irritation.

Meanwhile, Jessica argues with Todd on another part of the campus. She is furious that he left her party with Lannie last night.

"Who was she Todd?"

"Who?"

"Don't give me that! The slut at my birthday party. I didn't even invite her!"

"I don't know who you're talking about."

"Don't play dumb."

"Whatever. I'm going to class."

Todd walks away.

It is true. Jessica can be demanding. And Todd can be a jerk. They may or may not be perfect for each other. The pair are more alike than they will admit. After three years together, Todd is in love with Jessica, but currently in lust with Lannie. Lannie is different.

Lannie and Kellie sit in their dorm room. Lannie is dissatisfied. Kellie is happy. She hopes Lannie wants to stay at the university.

"Do you like it here yet," asked Kellie.

"It's okay," said Lannie.

"I really like Linc. There's a girl named Amy who likes him, too."

"Do you think he likes her?"

"He acts like he doesn't. But I can't tell if they have a history or not."

"You should enjoy Linc and spend as much time with him as you can. I'll take care of Amy."

"What are you going to do?"

"Don't worry about it. I said I'd take care of it."

Kellie smiles and is filled with excitement. She knows Lannie will help her. She knows Lannie will do something. Lannie will unleash wrath on Amy and that makes Kellie happy.

Amy is sweeping hair up from the floor and preparing to close when Lannie walks into the salon.

"I'm sorry. We're closed. I forgot to lock the door," said Amy.

Lannie walks through the salon looking around and not saying anything.

"You can come back tomorrow. We open at 10:00," said Amy.

Lannie picks up a pair of scissors.

"These are *very* shiny. I can almost see my reflection. Don't you think they're shiny," asked Lannie.

"Yeah, I guess. Do you go to CU? You look familiar."

"Why don't you sit down. I'll give you a haircut."

"No, thanks. I like my hair the way it is."

Lannie shoves Amy into a chair.

"Well, I don't!"

Lannie cuts Amy's hair. Amy starts
screaming.

"Stop! Why are you doing this?"

"Relax! You're going to look beautiful."

Amy starts crying.

"No! Stop!"

Lannie keeps quickly cutting Amy's hair then
cuts Amy's throat with the scissors.

The next day Simone waits for Jessica and
Amy in their usual meeting location on campus.
She notices they are both late, which is unusual.
Jay approaches Simone.

"Were you in class when I called," asked
Simone.

Jay kisses Simone.

"Yeah, but it was over. What's up," asked Jay.

"I'm not really sure. I was supposed to meet Jessica   and Amy, but they're not here."

"Maybe something came up."

"For both of them?"

Jay shrugs his shoulders and dreads the impending conversation. Simone is a natural caregiver. She wants to help everyone. She seeks solutions, so Jay knows if she is worried about something that is all they will discuss. Simone continues speaking.

"This is so not like either one of them. Are you hanging out with Todd tonight?"

"I don't know. I haven't heard from him yet."

Simone is suspicious.

"Oh."

"Oh, what?"

"Nothing."

"I don't hang out with the guy every day."

"I know. I just thought that since you guys are in the same fraternity…"

"Just because we're in the same frat doesn't mean anything. I moved out of that house for a reason."

"So you could study in peace."

"That's part of it."

"Why else?"

"It's been better for us."

"And?"

"That's all."

"I think there are other reasons that you will not discuss with me. I thought we wouldn't keep secrets from each other."

"You should know that I am up front with you. I have nothing to hide."

A student standing nearby Simone and Jay is talking to a friend. She tells her a girl from CU was found dead off campus today. Simone turns to her.

"Do you know who she was," asked Simone.

The student responds, "No, I wasn't given a name."

"Don't jump to conclusions," said Jay.

"Amy works off campus," said Simone.

"We still don't know if it was her or not."

Linc walks up to Simone and Jay.

"What's goin' on," asked Linc.

"Linc, have you seen Jessica or Amy," asked Simone.

"No. Have you seen Todd?"

"Jay hasn't heard from him today either."

Jay grows frustrated with Simone's inquiry.

"Stop jumping to conclusions!"

"I'm mad at him. He was supposed to meet me this morning and never showed. I'm sure I'll see him later at practice," said Linc.

"A dead body was found off campus. I just know it was Amy's," said Simone.

"No way!"

"We don't know if it was Amy's body that was found," said Jay.

"She's pledging for our sorority right now. Why would she ignore *me*," asked Simone.

"I'm sure you willhear from Jessica and Amy later," said Jay.

"I don't see why you can't understand!"

Simone is distressed with Jay and walks away.

"What is there to understand?

"What's wrong with her," asked Linc.

Jay does not respond to Linc or bother to run after Simone. The couple have been dating for two years and generally get along. He knows it is best to wait and let Simone calm down before speaking with her again.

Linc walks onto the football field and sees Todd with other teammates doing stretches on the field before practice and approaches him.

"Hey man, what happened to you this morning," asked Linc.

"Not you, too," said Todd.

"What's *that* supposed to mean?"

"Look, I'm dealing with enough right now. I don't need you checking up on me!"

"Dude! I don't care about checking up on you. We had plans."

Todd looks around, takes a deep breath, exhales, and then responds.

"Oh, yeah. We were supposed to look at the car, huh?"

"I really needed your help."

"I'm sorry, man. I'll make it up to you. I've been preoccupied with that Lannie chick. I can't figure her out."

"You like Lannie?"

"Yeah. How well do you know her?"

"Not really well. Just that she's Kellie's sister. What about Jessica?"

"What about her?"

"Are the two of you still together?"

"As of right now, yes, but not for much longer. Let's double date those two sisters some time."

Before Linc can respond, their coach yells for everyone to start practice.

That night Simone and Jay sit on a couch watching television in Jay's apartment. She is unsettled after overhearing students on campus talk about someone in town being murdered.

"I still haven't heard from Jessica or Amy. We talk *every* day," said Simone.

Jay tries to avoid a long conversation about this topic.

"Maybe they're mad at you," said Jay.

"Why would they be mad at me? All the sisters at the house are wondering where Jessica is."

Jay is distracted.

"Maybe they're playin' with you."

Simone is confused and turns to Jay.

"What? The only thing I can think of is that Amy didn't want Jessica to know that she works, and I sorta blurted it out the other day."

"Maybe that's it."

"Have you spoken to Todd today?"

"No."

"And you don't think that's strange?"

"No. I told you before. I don't talk to him every day. Something probably came up."

"Like what?"

"How am I supposed to know? I *do* know he's getting sick of Jessica. He probably just needed to get away."

"What do you mean he's getting sick of Jessica?"

"It's none of our business."

"She's my sister."

Jay grows even more annoyed by the discussion.

"You take that sorority crap too serious."

"It's not crap. Besides, you're in a fraternity."

"Yeah, and I do as less as possible."

"What happened between you guys?"

Jay does not respond. Simone continues.

"You put the Greek system down, yet you're protecting your brothers right now."

Jay gets up.

"No, Simone. I'm protecting you!"

Jay walks out of the room. He cannot bring himself to tell her what he knows about Todd and Lannie. Simone will tell Jessica and that will officially declare Simone a busybody. Jay does not gossip. He is a private person who purposely chooses to not get into the mix, which is why he moved out of the frat house. This causes him to operate on the surface, which annoys Simone because she wants him to open up.

The next day Simone steps outside of the sorority house and sees Jessica.

"Jessica!"

Jessica looks sad and does not immediately respond. Her face is moist from recent tears. Simone hugs her.

"Where have you been? We've been worried about you," said Simone.

"I had to get away," said Jessica.

"What's wrong?"

"Todd and I are finished."

"You guys broke up?"

"Well, it's not official yet. But soon we will be history."

"Is this what you want?"

Jessica starts crying again.

"No."

Simone puts her arm around Jessica.

"I've never seen you like this before. You're always so strong."

"He's involved with someone else . . . her name is Lannie or something."

"It's not like you to give up, Jessie. You should fight for him."

"It's no use. He's in love with her."

"It's ironic that I'm the one consoling you."

"What do you mean?"

"Jay and I got into a fight last night."

Jessica wants to continue talking about her issue with Todd and becomes irritated when Simone changes the subject. She pretends to care.

"Oh, no. About what?"

"I was worried about you and he just didn't get it. And you heard about Amy?"

"Amy, the pledge? No offense, but she's not right for us."

"Well, I don't know if it was her or not, but there was a dead body found off campus yesterday."

"In this town?"

"That's what people are saying."

"Why would you and Jay possibly be fighting about that?"

"That's just it. It's more than that. Ever since Jay got his apartment off campus he's been distant from his fraternity."

"Jay has a chip on his shoulder."

"What's that supposed to mean?"

"Nothing. It's just that the guys feel he thinks he's better than them."

"You knew about this?"

"Simone, don't be naïve. Everyone knows that   Jay and Todd's frat is the most vicious on campus. Jay's too strait-laced to get involved."

"I can't figure out why he ever joined."

"Maybe he changed."

Simone continues her quest to find out if Amy is the girl who was found dead. She meets

Linc at the campus Student Center for coffee,

hoping he can answer her questions.

"Did Todd ever call you yesterday," asked

Simone.

"No. I saw him at practice, though," said

Linc.

"How was he?"

"What do you mean?"

"Did he seem upset about anything?"

Linc becomes annoyed with Simone's

questions.

"I don't know. Why?"

"Jessica came home this morning, and she

was pretty torn up."

Linc's annoyance turns to curiosity.

"About what?"

"She thinks Todd is going to break up with her."

Kellie walks into the Student Center. She sees Linc talking to Simone and is overflowing with jealously. When Kellie sees Professor Davis, she walks over to her and sits down. Professor Davis notices how uncomfortable Kellie is and asks if she is okay. Kellie does not respond, gets up and walks over to Linc and Simone.

"Hi Linc," said Kellie.

"Hi Kellie," said Linc as he places a kiss on her cheek. "Do you know Simone?"

"No."

"Hi Kellie," said Simone.

Still brimming with jealously, Kellie turns to Linc.

"Linc, are you still coming over tonight? Lannie will be at the library."

"Of course. I'll be over."

"Okay, great. I'll see you then. It was nice meeting   you Simone."

Kellie quickly walks away.

Simone senses Kellie's uneasiness, forces a smile, and continues talking as Kellie walks away.

"It was nice meeting you," said Simone.

Kellie hesitates before continuing her exit. Simone thinks the encounter is strange and returns to the conversation she and Linc were having before Kellie's abrupt appearance.

"I have got to find out where Amy is," said Simone.

"Well, when you find out let me know. I'm pretty curious myself," said Linc.

"You know, she really likes you."

"No, I didn't know that."

"You can't tell?"

"No."

"Well, she does."

Linc is unsure of how to react.

"What's the story with you and Kellie?"

"There is no story. We're a couple."

"You hardly know her."

"And we're getting to know each other."

"What's the deal with that girl she came to Jessica's party with?"

"You mean Lannie?"

"Yeah. Jessica's really angry with her."

"I don't know much about Lannie."

"Well, you do know that she slept with Todd on Jessica's birthday."

"No, I didn't know that."

Linc starts feeling uncomfortable with the conversation and stands up.

"Simone, I've gotta go."

"Bye."

"See ya."

Two of Simone's sorority sisters, Claudia and Yancy, are in the sorority house living room. Yancy is on her phone reading an article on the local newspaper's Website. Suddenly, she is alarmed and begins reading aloud.

"Amy Estes, a freshman at California University, was found brutally murdered yesterday at a hair salon near the CU campus."

"No way! The Amy who's pledging our sorority," asked Claudia.

"Yes, that's what it says."

Simone enters the living room.

"What's up," asks Simone.

"Amy was murdered," said Claudia.

"No," said Simone.

"It says so right here," said Yancy.

Yancy holds up her phone and hands it to Simone, who quickly grabs it and falls onto the couch next to Yancy.

"I knew it was her! This is awful," said Simone.

Simone is deeply saddened and Yancy is in shock.

"Who would do this to her," asked Claudia.

The room is silent. Simone starts crying. Yancy is speechless.

"I don't know," said Simone.

After a moment, Yancy speaks again.

"We should do something."

"Like what," asked Claudia.

"I'm not sure. It just seems like we should make a statement or do something. I don't know."

"You're right. Let's have a meeting with all the sisters tonight," said Simone.

Meanwhile, on campus Jessica sees Lannie and walks up to her.

"Are you aware that Todd is unavailable," asked Jessica.

"Yeah, so," asked Lannie.

Jessica cannot believe her arrogance and struggles with a response.

"What do you mean, yeah so?"

"Look, if Todd's your boyfriend I'm happy for you."

Jessica is confused.

"Didn't the two of you spend the night together?"

"What's it to you?"

"He's *my* man."

"Didn't we already establish that?"

"I don't get you. He's mine and I want you to stay away from him!"

"I'm not interested in forming a *relationship* with *your* boyfriend. We just had sex."

Jessica's confusion turns to anger, and she shouts as Lannie walks away.

"Stay away from Todd!"

Jessica storms into the sorority house where everyone is saddened by the news of Amy's murder.

"What's wrong," asked Jessica.

"Amy was murdered," said Simone.

"Amy. . .the pledge?"

"Yeah."

"No offense, but she was not right for us. I keep telling you that."

"She was murdered!"

"I heard you the first time! I'm sorry, but what can *we* do? We can't bring her back!"

"What's wrong with you?"

Jessica grows even more frustrated.

"I just talked with that Lannie person."

"How'd it go?"

"She's a bitch! She claims that she just slept with Todd one time and I shouldn't worry about it."

"What? That sounds sleazy."

"She *is* sleazy. I don't like her. I have no idea what Todd sees in her."

"Neither do I, but it may just be sex."

"You make it sound like you approve."

"No, I don't. I just can't believe it."

Jessica softens her voice.

"Do you think he'll see her again?"

"I don't know. Have you talked to him?"

"He won't listen to me."

Jessica hears several sorority sisters talking in a nearby room.

"Are we having a meeting," asked Jessica.

"The sisters want to plan a memorial service for Amy."

Simone and Jessica walk into the living room, sit down, and join their sisters in the meeting.

Chapter 5

Turning Point

Kellie and Lannie sit in their dorm room. Kellie is apprehensive because Lannie is sitting next to her but seems distant.

"Linc is coming over soon," said Kellie

"I'm on my way out," said Lannie

"Good. I told him you would be at the library."

Lannie does not like this. She believes she is being pushed aside and being replaced by Linc. She fakes an interest in what Kellie is saying.

"How are things going for you two?"

"Good, I guess. I didn't   see Amy around him today. But he was talking to some   chick named Simone."

Now Lannie is interested in this discussion.

"Do you think she likes him?"

"No, Simone seems really nice. I think she has a boyfriend."

Lannie is envious of Kellie.

"You're making a lot of friends."

Lannie gets up. Kellie is confused. Linc walks into the room as Lannie walks out. He speaks to her, but Lannie doesn't say anything.

"Hi Linc!"

Linc kisses Kellie.

"What's wrong with her?"

"Nothing's wrong."

"Today has certainly been strange."

"Forget Lannie. She's always like that."

Linc sits down on the bed next to Kellie.

"Whatever. You know that girl I was talking to today, Simone?"

"Yeah."

"She's totally worried because one of her sorority's pledges is missing."

"So. Why do you care about that?"

"Normally I wouldn't, but she went on and on about it. And yesterday she heard that a dead body was found off campus."

"A dead body?"

"Yeah. Haven't you heard?"

This *is* news for Kellie. She does not share her strong suspicion that Lannie is probably responsible for it. Now she understands Lannie's behavior.

"You just told me."

"Simone is very upset about it."

"Stop talking about her!"

"You don't have to be jealous of Simone. She's been with Jay for two years. She and I are just. . ."

Kellie does not let Linc finish his sentence.

"Just what?"

"We're trying to figure out if Amy is dead or missing."

"Amy?"

"Yeah, that's who's missing."

Kellie conceals her happiness.

"So what if she's dead?" Let's talk about something else."

Kellie sits on Linc's lap and kisses him.

"You don't think death is serious?"

"I do. But I didn't know her very well.

"You're being insensitive."

"Huh? No, I just want to be with you right now and not talk. I care about people."

"Okay."

Linc quickly kisses Kellie and starts talking again.

"You know, I can't get my mind off something Todd said earlier today."

Kellie moves even closer to Linc.

"Well, I'll help you get your mind off of it."

Linc stands up.

"What's wrong with you?"

"Nothing. I just wish you would stop talking."

Linc starts feeling uncomfortable, changes the subject, and eventually sits down again.

"Todd wants us to double date so he can go out with Lannie."

"Really? That can be arranged."

"Do you think Lannie will go for it?"

"I'll ask her."

Linc's phone rings in his pocket. Kellie is impatient and jumps up.

"Another interruption!"

Linc answers the call.

"Hello. Oh, no way. Let me know if you need anything. Bye."

"Who was that?"

Linc responds slowly.

"It was Simone. She found out it was Amy's body that was found yesterday. She was murdered."

"Really? How does *she* know? Amy could have killed herself."

"It was on the local newspaper's Website. Besides, Amy would never do that."

"How do you know?"

"She just wouldn't. I can't figure out who would do something like this."

Kellie starts pacing then turns to Linc.

"You liked her."

"Of course, I liked her."

"Before you said you didn't."

Linc is confused.

"What? I meant that she was a good friend. I wasn't attracted to her at all."

Kellie calms down, sits down on Linc's lap, and puts her arms around him.

"Oh. Well, she really liked you. Where were we?

Linc pulls away and stands up.

"Kellie, I can't do this tonight."

Kellie stands up.

"Why not?"

"I just can't. I'll see you tomorrow."

Linc leaves the room and Lannie walks in shortly after.

"Did you kill Amy?"

"Who's Amy," asked Lannie.

"Answer me. Did you kill anyone?"

By the look on Lannie's face, Kellie can tell that the answer is *yes*.

"You said that she was in the way."

"I told you I was trying to make friends. Now Linc is preoccupied with her murder!"

Lannie partially smiles.

"Oh. Well, maybe he's not worth it."

"What do you mean?"

"I mean, maybe you shouldn't get involved with him."

Kellie gets upset.

"I really like him. If you do anything to hurt him, I swear, I will kill you!"

"You could never do it."

Kellie steps closer to Lannie.

"Try me!"

Lannie slaps Kellie.

"Don't *ever* talk to me like that!"

Kellie cries, goes to her side of the room, and lies down, turning away from Lannie.

The next evening, Todd and Linc are standing outside of a restaurant, waiting for Lannie and Kellie.

"I thought you said Lannie and her sister would be here," said Todd.

"They will," said Linc.

"Where are they?"

"They will be here."

Todd continues waiting impatiently. Then suddenly Kellie and Lannie arrive.

"I'm sorry we're late," said Kellie.

Todd walks up to Lannie.

"Hi Lannie," said Todd.

"What's the point of this," asked Lannie.

"I want to spend time with you."

"Why?"

Todd is confused.

"Do you ever let your guard down?"

"No, why?"

"You guys, let's go inside," said Linc.

Lannie and Todd walk inside the restaurant. Kellie is worried and blocks the doorway so Linc is forced to stop walking.

"Are you still mad at me," asked Kellie.

"I was never mad. I just thought you were acting weird," said Linc.

Kellie kisses Linc.

"I'm sorry."

"It's okay."

While eating dinner Kellie stares at Linc obsessively. She makes him uncomfortable. Lannie focuses on ignoring Todd as he moves his chair even closer to her.

Later, when the quartet exits the restaurant Linc tells Todd he and Kellie are walking back to campus. Todd informs him that he and Lannie are going for a drive, and she overhears, as Linc and Kellie walk away.

"We are," asked Lannie.

"Yeah, don't you want to hang out," asked Todd.

"Not really."

"I know you like me."

"And how do you know that?"

Todd moves closer to Lannie.

"This hard-to-get routine…typical."

"I'm not playing hard to get."

"Then what are you doing?"

"I'm walking home."

Todd grabs Lannie's arm.

"I know you like me."

Lannie pulls her arm back.

"No, I don't."

"I like you."

"No one likes me except Kellie. She's the nice one. Why don't you like her? Everyone else does."

"Because you're the one I want."

Lannie moves closer to Todd and kisses him.

"See, I knew you liked me."

Lannie smiles.

The next day Jay is walking on campus and approaches Simone. She verbally responds to him but is emotionally distant.

"Are you mad at me," asked Jay. "I haven't seen or heard from you in two days."

"I was, but not anymore," said Simone.

Simone informs Jay that the girl who was murdered the other night was Amy. Everyone on campus is talking about it, so Jay is more understanding of Simone's feelings. He hugs Simone and apologizes for his behavior because he knows she really liked Amy.

When Linc approaches Jay and Simone, Jay tells him about Amy because he believes Simone is unable to say the words, *Amy's dead*. He is surprised to learn Simone and Linc have already been discussing it.

"Nothing like this ever happens here," said Linc.

"How would you know," asked Jay. "You're a freshman."

"I read this was a safe place. No crime."

"Well, times have changed."

"You don't think this could happen again, do you," asked Simone.

"I don't know. But none of us are safe until they catch whoever did this," said Jay.

"Don't you think they've left town by now," asked Linc.

"Maybe," said Jay.

"I sure hope so," said Simone.

Later in the freshman dormitory, Linc enters Kellie's room. After talking with Simone and Jay about Amy he decides to check in on her. He hugs her immediately.

"I missed you. I don't want anything to happen to you," said Linc.

Kellie is confused by Linc's behavior.

"Why are you talking like this," asked Kellie.

"I can't believe what happened to Amy."

Kellie turns around and walks away from Linc. Then she yells at him.

"There's nothing we can do about it. She's dead!"

"Kellie, you're being insensitive again. Are you okay?"

"I'm fine! I just wish you would stop talking about *those people*."

"What do you mean *those people*?"

"You care more about them than me."

"That's not true."

"You keep talking about them!"

Kellie is enraged and starts hitting Linc. Linc grabs Kellie.

"I'm outta here! You're crazy," said Linc.

Linc walks away. Kellie pushes him, bangs his head against the wall, and he falls to the floor. She bends down and shakes him, but he is unresponsive. Lannie enters the room. Kellie is in the fetal position in a corner and crying. Lannie sees Linc is dead on the floor. She walks over to Kellie.

"Don't worry. I will take care of this," said Lannie.

"Why did you kill Amy," asked Kellie.

"I told you I would take   care of everything."

"I liked Amy. I just didn't want her to take Linc away from me. Linc. Oh, no! What have I done?"

Lannie forces Kellie to sit up.

"Pull yourself together!   We need to get him out of here. These people are taking you away from me."

Lannie and Kellie take Linc's body outside and Simone sees them. They see her, too. The two sisters put down Linc's body and chase Simone.

"Go that way," said Lannie.

Lannie and Kellie run in different directions. Lannie purposely sends Kellie the wrong way because she believes Simone will be easy to deal with later. Her anger and behavior are arranged like a task list. She prioritizes, so there is a method for her actions and she can justify them without feeling remorseful.

"Where is she," asked Kellie.

"She got away," said Lannie.

"That was Simone."

"Forget her! Let's get to work."

Jay is asleep on the couch in his apartment when he hears knocking at the door. He slowly gets up then opens the door.

"What's going on," asked Jay.

Simone is upset. It takes a moment, but she regains her composure.

"You're never going to believe this. I saw Kellie and her sister carrying what looked like a body," said Simone.

"Yeah, right. So was it?"

"I don't know. It was dark. I couldn't see."

"Well, so what? Maybe they're pledging for a sorority or something."

"No. I think it's much more serious than that."

"Stop making such a big deal out of this!"

Jay sits down on the couch and Simone starts crying. She sits next to him, and he tries to console her.

"This isn't right. I just know something terrible has happened."

"Are you sure it was a body?"

"I'm scared."

"Don't worry. You're safe with me."

The next day Simone walks around campus terrified, angry, and sad. Lannie and Kellie see her.

"Go talk to Simone," said Lannie.

"Why," asked Kellie. "What am I supposed to say to her?"

"Just be friendly. You're good at that."

Kellie walks up to Simone and startles her. Kellie smiles and Simone is afraid. Jay walks up to them and Simone runs away. Kellie is very angry. Jay sees the look in Kellie's eyes and walks backward, eventually turning around and running away himself.

Simone runs directly into Lannie.

"Hi Simone," said Lannie.

Simone starts crying.

"What's wrong? You look scared," said Lannie.

Lannie puts her arm around Simone and pulls her. Kellie sees them and assists Lannie with forcing Simone to walk with them.

Lannie and Kellie tie up Simone and take her off campus to a nearby canyon.

"You should really mind your own business," said Lannie.

Simone is crying and very confused.

"What are you talking about," asked Simone.

"Don't be stupid," said Kellie.

"I don't know what you're talking about," said Simone.

"You're starting to become a problem for us," said Lannie.

"Please let me go. I won't tell anyone about you," said Simone.

"Simone, why should we trust you," asked Lannie.

"I can't stand you! I'll never trust you," said Kellie.

"Please let me go," said Simone.

Lannie and Kellie continue yelling at Simone, then they stab her. Simone dies and the two sisters walk away.

Lannie and Kellie return to their dorm room. Kellie is scared but Lannie is calm.

"We should leave this place," said Kellie.

"Are you crazy," asked Lannie.

"I thought you hated it here."

"I do. But we can't leave *now*."

"Why not?"

"Do you want to go back to Standard?"

"Hell no!"

"Then you better get used to this place."

"I'm going for a walk. Maybe I can seduce Todd again."

"You really like him, huh?"

"He's okay."

Lannie smiles and walks out of the room.

As Lannie approaches Todd's frat house, she sees him outside talking with Jessica. They are arguing. Todd gets into his car and starts the engine.

"Look, Jessica, I told you it was over. I've had it," said Todd.

"I can accept that we're over, but I cannot accept you hanging out

with that sleazy girl," said Jessica.

Jessica walks away and Todd jumps out of his car to follow her.

"What is that supposed to mean?"

"Just wait until your parents find out you're dating a nobody."

Todd grabs Jessica.

"And how are they going to find out?"

Jessica starts crying.

"I won't say anything."

Lannie suddenly goes into a jealous rage. She gets inside Todd's car and chases Todd and Jessica, who run for their lives. Lannie succeeds in running them over. She stops the car, gets out, and walks away.

After class Jay takes out his cell phone and calls Simone. When there is no answer, he walks to the sorority house. On the way, he sees a crowd of people in the street.

"What's going on," asked Jay.

"Someone ran over Todd Williams and Jessica Garner," said a university student.

Jay is confused.

"What do you mean ran over?"

"With a car. They're both dead."

"Dead?"

"Yeah, somebody must have been *really* drunk."

"Please stand back! Better yet, leave this area," said Detective Thomas Riley.

Chapter 6

Detective Crawford

The next day Jay walks to Simone's sorority house. Yancy answers the door.

"Jay, what are you doing here," asked Yancy.

"I want to see Simone. Is she here," asked Jay.

"No, we thought she was with you."

"Did she say where she was going?"

"We haven't seen her since yesterday. She didn't come home last night."

Jay is confused.

"Jay, what's wrong," asked Yancy.

"Thanks."

Jays walks away. He is confused and gets upset. He goes to the campus police station. He starts talking to the first person he sees.

"I want to file a missing person's report," said Jay.

"What seems to be the problem," asked the receptionist.

"My girlfriend is missing."

"How long has she been missing?"

"One day."

"Well, give me her name, and if something comes up I'll let you know."

"That's it?"

"She's only been missing for a day. What exactly do you want us to do?"

"I want you to help me find her. Forget it. I'm going to the real police."

Jay runs out of the building.

At the city police station Detective Crawford is in her office when Detective Riley walks into the room and hands her a report.

"We just got this report from some kid named Jay about his girlfriend missing," said Detective Riley.

"How long has she been gone," asked Detective Crawford.

"He said about a day."

Detective Crawford looks at the report, smiles, and makes a determination.

"Lovers quarrel. They're going to kiss and make up and it's all going to go away."

Detective Riley smiles as Detective Crawford puts the report on her desk.

"Okay."

After they finish talking, Detective Crawford's telephone rings. She answers and has a brief conversation, then gets up and leaves. She goes to a canyon near the California University campus.

That night the canyon has become a crime scene investigation with several police officers, the coroner, Detective Riley, and Detective Crawford present. They have found Simone's body.

"She was tied up. She had been stabbed several times and brutally tortured. We think she knew her attacker," said Detective Riley.

"Do you think there was only one person who did this," asked Detective Crawford.

"We don't know yet. It's possible there could have been two people. Do you think there is a connection to the body we found at the hair salon and the two in the street?"

"That's what I'm going to find out. In the meantime, get a grid going, bag the evidence, and don't miss anything."

The next day Yancy is jogging in her neighborhood. When she returns to the sorority house, Claudia is sitting in the front yard.

"How was your run," asked Claudia.

"Good," said Yancy.

Detective Crawford walks up to them, shows her badge, tells them she has sad news and prefers to speak with them inside. Yancy and Claudia walk Detective Crawford into the house and they sit down.

"One of your sisters has been murdered," said Detective Crawford.

"Who," asked Claudia.

"Simone Reaves."

Claudia starts crying.

"How did this happen? Who did this," asked Yancy.

"That's why I'm here. I need your help. Do you know if she had any enemies," asked Detective Crawford.

"No. Everybody likes Simone," said Claudia.

"Can you think of any reason why someone would want to do this to her?"

"No."

"What about Jessica Garner?"

"She's dead, too," said Yancy.

"Her body was found yesterday. It was a hit and run," said Detective Crawford.

"We heard about it. But still can't believe it's true. I remember Simone thought it was strange that Jessica was gone a few days ago, but we just thought she went somewhere with Todd. After that Jessica came back okay," said Claudia.

"Todd Williams was her boyfriend," asked Detective Crawford.

"Yeah."

"Everybody likes Jessica, too. She's really confident and stuff," said Yancy.

Claudia cannot believe Yancy would say that. She takes Detective Crawford's investigation seriously, so she decides total honesty is best.

"Some people think she's arrogant. And she unfortunately does have some enemies," said Claudia.

"Do you know any of them," asked Detective Crawford.

"There's a new girl named Lannie. She slept with Todd, and it really made Jessica angry. They argued a lot and broke up over it."

"Yeah. Lannie's weird. And her sister Kellie is, too. They live in the dorms. We liked Kellie until she took Linc away from Amy," said Yancy.

"Amy Estes," asked Detective Crawford.

"Yes," said Yancy.

Detective Crawford is pleased with the information Yancy and Claudia have provided. She believes they have given good leads so she stands up and prepares to leave.

"Thank you, ladies. You've been very helpful."

As soon as Detective Crawford exits the house, Yancy and Claudia start talking.

"Why did you tell the detective that Jessica was arrogant and had enemies," asked Yancy.

"Because it's the truth. Jessica treated everyone like shit and
you know it," said Claudia.

"Are you glad she's dead?"

"I didn't say that."

Detective Crawford does not waste any time. She immediately follows Yancy and Claudia's lead and investigates Lannie and Kellie. After finding out which dormitory they live in, she goes inside the building. A student walking down the hall tells her where their room is located.

Detective Crawford tries opening the door and it is unlocked so she enters the room, looks around, does not see anything too strange, and then Kellie arrives. She is wearing a robe and has a towel wrapped around her head.

"Who are you," asked Kellie.

Detective Crawford shows Kellie her badge and introduces herself.

"What are you doing *here*," asked Kellie.

"Do you know Simone Reaves," asked Detective Crawford.

"No. I don't know very many people. I just moved here."

"How about Amy Estes? Do you know her?"

Kellie starts shaking and sweating.

"I don't know what you're talking about."

Detective Crawford tries to get Kellie to open up.

"The word on campus is, you've been dating her boyfriend, Linc."

Detective Crawford's strategy works. Kellie is instantly irritated.

"Linc is *my* boyfriend. I don't know who Amy is."

Lannie enters the room.

"Who are you," asked Lannie.

Detective Crawford shows Lannie her badge and introduces herself.

"I'm investigating two homicides that occurred near campus," said Detective Crawford.

"We wouldn't know anything about that. We just moved here."

"Yeah, that's what your sister told me."

"How did you know we were sisters?"

"Lucky guess."

"I think you should get out of here."

"All right. Be sure to call me if you think of anything."

Detective Crawford exits the room and Kellie is worried.

"Who do you think told the police about us," asked Kellie.

"I don't know yet, but when I find out. . .," said Lannie.

Before Lannie can complete her sentence, Kellie impatiently asks her a question.

"Why did she say two murders?"

"I have no idea."

While walking across campus, Detective Crawford stops and reaches inside her pocket. She takes out a pen she wrapped in plastic while in Lannie and Kellie's room. She goes inside a building where she is told Jay may be for a class. When she enters the classroom, Jay is alone. He sits at a desk crying and praying.

"Where could she be," asked Jay, not expecting anyone to hear.

"Jay," asked Detective Crawford.

Jay stands up and shakes Detective Crawford's hand.

"I have some sad news. We found Simone's body," said Detective Crawford."

"Is she dead?"

"Yes."

Jay sits down and Detective Crawford sits next to him.

"Who did this?"

"That's what we're trying to find out. I need your help. Did Simone have any enemies?"

"No. Everyone loves . . . I mean loved her."

"Can you think of any reason why someone would do this to her?"

"No."

"If you think of anything, give me a call."

"Okay."

Detective Crawford gives Jay her business card, gets up and walks away. Then Jay gets up and stops her.

"The other night Simone said that she saw two sisters on campus, Lannie and Kellie, carrying what looked like a body."

"Did she say whose body?"

"No. I didn't even believe her at first."

In a lecture hall Kellie sits in Professor Davis's class. She looks at the empty seat next to her and starts thinking about Linc. She gets up and runs out of the room.

As soon as Detective Crawford returns to the police station, she hands Detective Riley the pen she picked up in Lannie and Kellie's dorm room. She requests prints and DNA analysis.

At his apartment Jay calls Linc. He gets his voicemail. He leaves Linc a message, telling him to call as soon as he can because there is bad news about Simone.

In the dormitory dining commons Kellie questions Lannie about information she has discovered.

"There was a hit and run accident the other night. Would you know anything about that," asked Kellie.

"Maybe," said Lannie.

"What do you mean maybe?   You told me that you did not want to go back to Standard. But if you keep   this up, that's where we're going."

"I told you to never talk to me like that!"

A student sitting nearby stares at the two sisters as they raise their voices. Lannie yells at him.

"What are you lookin' at," asked Lannie.

"I thought we were a team," said Kellie.

"We are."

"Then why are you acting like I'm against you?"

"I don't have to answer to you."

"You killed Amy. We both killed Simone."

"You killed your beloved Linc."

"That's not fair! Why did you run over Jessica and Todd?"

"I didn't care about Todd. And he didn't care about me. Jessica just got in the way."

Lannie smiles as she says Jessica's name.

"So what do we do now?"

"I told you I would take   care of everything."

"I know. You have been saying that and all these things are happening. We need to do something. That detective is onto us."

"We can't leave."

"Why not?"

"It's too suspicious."

"Lannie, they're already onto us. Let's go away. They'll *never* find us."

"I think I know who told the detective about us. And I know what we're going to do."

At the police station Detective Crawford discovers that Lannie and Kellie were once mental patients. Detective Riley also informs her that the prints she gave him match the ones on the scissors at the salon and the car. She calls Dr. Henderson at Standard Sanitarium, but he is unavailable, so she speaks with Nurse Louise Brennan.

"This is Detective Crawford with Municipal P.D. I'm conducting an investigation. Do you remember patients Lannie and Kellie Ryan?"

"Yes, I know them both very well," said Nurse Louise.

"Why were they institutionalized?"

"When they were 13 and 14 they killed their aunt. Their uncle was terrified of them. They suffer from manic depression."

"How long were they at Standard?"

"For five years. And if you ask me, that was not long enough. Both of them should be locked up for the rest of their lives."

"Do you think they pose a threat to society?"

"Absolutely, especially if they are not taking their meds."

"What medications are they taking?"

"Lithium. I tried telling Dr. Henderson, but he wouldn't listen to me. Have they gotten into trouble?"

"At California University in just the past few weeks two students were murdered and two others were mysteriously killed in a hit and run accident. Does that sound like something they would do?"

"Detective, you had better take both of them into custody immediately. They're a threat to themselves and to others. Should I tell Dr. Henderson to call you?"

"Thank you for your time. I will be contacting him."

Chapter 7

Conclusion

Yancy, Claudia, and their sorority sisters host an outdoor ceremony on campus so everyone can have an opportunity to pay their respects to Simone, Jessica, and Amy. Yancy and Claudia are standing behind a podium as people gather. Jay is in attendance. He cannot believe Lannie and Kellie are there.

"We know that you all are aware of the recent events that have plagued our campus and town. Unfortunately, we have lost two of our sisters and a pledge who we loved. Join us in a moment of silence," said Claudia.

Everyone bows their heads during the prayer except for Lannie. Instead, she looks around.

"Is that him," asked Lannie.

"Yes, that's Jay. Simone was his girlfriend," said Kellie.

"Go talk to him."

"Why?"

"Just do it. I'll go with you."

After the ceremony ends some people stand around talking. Kellie slowly approaches Jay.

"Hi Jay. I'm sorry about what happened to Simone," said Kellie.

"Yeah, me too," said Jay.

"This is my sister, Lannie."

"Sorry about your loss," said Lannie.

"Why are you two here," asked Jay.

"What do you mean," asked Kellie.

Professor Davis is close by and listens to this conversation. Nurse Louise from Standard Sanitarium also walks up behind Lannie and Kellie at this time.

"I don't know. You tell me. For some reason Simone was afraid of you," said Jay.

Lannie laughs.

"Afraid of us," asked Lannie.

"Yeah. I don't know what you did, but I know it was wrong. Simone

would never lie to me."

"Well, now she can never do that again."

Jay cannot believe what he is hearing. Lannie's insensitivity disturbs him. He shakes his head and walks away.

"Hello girls," said Nurse Louise.

Lannie and Kellie are shocked! California University is supposed to be a place that takes them away from their past. Now the life they never want to remember is standing right in front of them.

"Nurse Louise! What are you doing here," asked Kellie.

"I was about to ask you the same thing," said Nurse Louise.

"We don't have to talk to you. We're free of you now. Come on Kellie," said Lannie.

Lannie grabs Kellie's arm and begins walking away. She stops when Nurse Louise continues speaking.

"Lannie, I'm concerned about you. That's all," said Nurse Louise.

"Concerned? How did you even know where to find us," asked Lannie.

This time Lannie walks away pulling Kellie with her. Nurse Louise is disappointed and feels helpless. Her suspicions about Lannie and Kellie are confirmed but she believes she is incapable of helping them. Professor Davis walks up to her and they shake hands.

"Hi. I'm Renee' Davis."

"Louise Brennan. Do you know Lannie and Kellie Ryan?"

"Kellie is in one of my English Literature classes. She's a good student. She seems like a nice person, even though she is a bit strange."

"A bit strange. What do you mean?"

"It appears that she has a lot of friends, but she does not. . .I don't know. I can't really put my finger on it. I noticed that she has lost weight and often falls asleep during my lectures."

Professor Davis stops talking and laughs.

"But several students do that from time to time," said Professor Davis.

"Have you noticed anything else?"

"Only that when I have worked with her one-on-one she became irritable at times. Why? Is there something you're not telling me?"

"Renee', all I can really tell you is that Kellie is not well."

"Should I be afraid?"

"Unfortunately, yes."

Later that evening Nurse Louise walks to her car in one of the campus parking lots. On the way she hears a noise. Suddenly, Lannie and Kellie come up behind her and choke her until she dies.

After thinking about her conversation with Nurse Louise, Detective Crawford calls Jay, but the telephone just rings. She decides to go see Jay in person and tell him about Lannie and Kellie.

At Jay's apartment, he steps out of his bedroom, walks into the living room, and sees Lannie sitting on his couch. She offers him a sinister smile, he tries to escape, but Kellie runs up behind him with a knife and stabs him in the shoulder.

"What the. . .awww! The police are onto you guys," said Jay.

"We should have killed you first," said Lannie.

Jay, Lannie and Kellie wrestle because Jay puts up a physical struggle. Kellie drops the knife. Detective Crawford approaches the front door and hears a loud noise. As a result, she storms into the apartment and shoots Kellie while she tries reaching for the knife. Kellie dies.

Lannie is still beating Jay. She looks up and sees Detective Crawford and runs towards her with a knife. Lannie wrestles with Detective Crawford, who drops her gun.

Jay is weak, falls to the ground, and slowly crawls towards Detective Crawford's gun. He shoots the gun several times before finally hitting Lannie. She falls and dies instantly.

The outside of Jay's apartment is now a crime scene investigation with police officers, emergency medical technicians, the coroner, and Detective Crawford present. Jay receives medical attention for his wounds.

"I can't believe any of this happened," said Jay.

"I'm sorry you had to go through all this," said Detective Crawford.

"So Lannie and Kellie are the ones who killed Simone?"

"Yes. And Amy, Jessica, and Todd."

"I can't believe this."

"You were smart to come to us when you did."

Detective Crawford walks away from Jay. He calls for her and she turns around and walks back to him.

"Can you help me again?"

"Sure."

"My friend Linc is missing. I haven't seen him for a few days. I left him a message and he still hasn't called me back. It's not like him."

While Jay is speaking, Detective Crawford's phone rings, she answers, and it is Detective Riley.

"Crawford here."

"We found two more bodies on campus."

Detective Crawford goes to the California University campus. Law enforcement vehicles and ambulances cover the main entrance of the school. School staff and students are on lockdown. The university chancellor agrees with law enforcement that as few people as possible should witness the emergency response. Detective Crawford walks over to the ambulances and sees two body bags. She speaks with the officers. The two bodies match descriptions for Linc and Nurse Louise Brennan.